★ *GREAT SPORTS TEAMS* ★

THE BALTIMORE

BASEBALL TEAM

David Pietrusza

```
RENFROE MIDDLE SCHOOL
220 WEST COLLEGE AVE.
DECATUR, GEORGIA 30030
```

Enslow Publishers, Inc.
40 Industrial Road   PO Box 38
Box 398   Aldershot
Berkeley Heights, NJ 07922 Hants GU12 6BP
USA   UK
     http://www.enslow.com

To Pearl Pietrusza LaMalfa

Copyright © 2000 by Enslow Publishers, Inc.

All rights reserved.

No part of this book may be reproduced by any means without the written permission of the publisher.

Library of Congress Cataloging-in-Publication Data

Pietrusza, David, 1949–
    The Baltimore Orioles baseball team / David Pietrusza.
       p. cm. — (Great sports teams)
    Includes bibliographical references and index.
    Summary: Describes the history of the Baltimore Orioles from the early twentieth century to the early 1990s, highlighting the key personalities and memorable games.
    ISBN 0-7660-1283-2
    1. Baltimore Orioles (Baseball team)—History Juvenile literature.
[1. Baltimore Orioles (Baseball team)—History. 2. Baseball—History.]
I. Title. II. Series.
GV875.B2P54   2000
796.357'64'097526—dc21   99-30156
                                                                       CIP

Printed in the United States of America

10 9 8 7 6 5 4 3 2 1

To Our Readers: All Internet addresses in this book were active and appropriate when we went to press. Any comments or suggestions can be sent by e-mail to Comments@enslow.com or to the address on the back cover.

Illustration Credits: AP/Wide World Photos.

Cover Illustration: AP/Wide World Photos.

Cover Description: Cal Ripken, Jr.

CONTENTS

1 The Iron Man 5

2 Before Baltimore 11

3 Orioles Immortals 17

4 Orioles Management 23

5 A Winning Tradition 29

6 Roller-Coaster Change 35

Statistics 40

Chapter Notes 43

Glossary 44

Further Reading 46

Index 47

Where to Write 48

As Cal Ripken, Jr., was nearing the record, the number of his consecutive games played was displayed on the B&O warehouse behind right field at Camden Yards.

THE IRON MAN

For decades it had seemed to be the unbreakable record—Lou Gehrig's consecutive-games-played streak of 2,130 straight contests. Gehrig had played with the New York Yankees season after season, through injury and fatigue, until he was tragically cut down by a fatal disease. Since his passing, his record had seemed unbreakable. "Larrupin' Lou" had set the mark in 1939. The closest any player had come to breaking it was a mere 1,207 games by Dodgers and Padres first baseman Steve Garvey.

Not very close at all.

A New Challenger

Then sometime around 1990 people began noticing something was up. Baltimore's All-Star shortstop, Cal Ripken, Jr., had played in every Orioles game since May 30, 1982. He began the streak as a third baseman. Game after game, year after year, he remained in the lineup. During the 1990 season, he played in his

1,308th straight game and passed shortstop Everett Scott for second place on the all-time list. But not everyone was cheering for Ripken—and they were not all Lou Gehrig fans. Some observers questioned whether Ripken was helping—or hurting—his team. "Ripken's pursuit [of the record] is counterproductive both to himself and his team," wrote baseball analyst Steve Hirdt.[1] By the time a players strike ended the 1994 season, Ripken was clearly within distance of Gehrig, having played in 2,009 consecutive games.

No Replacement

Major League owners threatened to start the 1995 season with "replacement" players. Ripken vowed that he would not cross the union's picket line and play with the "replacements." Officially, his streak could have come to an end. But then Orioles owner Peter Angelos promised he would never field a "replacement" team. The strike was settled. Play began again—and "The Streak" replaced "The Strike."

On September 5, 1995, Ripken played in his 2,130th straight contest, tying Gehrig's mark. The next night 46,272 fans crowded into Baltimore's beautiful new stadium, Oriole Park at Camden Yards. Across America millions of fans cheered the event on television.

Ripken again was in the starting lineup. To add to the excitement, he homered in the fourth inning. The record, however, would not become official until the game itself became official in the middle of the fifth inning. When Orioles second baseman Manny Alexander caught Angel Damion Easley's pop-up to end the

The Baltimore Orioles Baseball Team

In the 1920s and 1930s, Lou Gehrig played in 2,130 consecutive games. For many years, that record was believed to be unbreakable.

top of the fifth inning, it made the game official. Ripken now held the record.

The Celebration Begins

Alexander's catch triggered a wild, unprecedented twenty-two minute, fifteen second, standing ovation for Ripken. Teammates and opponents jogged over to

The Iron Man

After officially breaking Gehrig's record on September 6, 1995, Cal Ripken, Jr., took a victory lap around Oriole Park at Camden Yards, shaking hands with as many people as he could.

the new record holder to congratulate him. Fireworks went off. Ripken hugged his wife and children and then his mother and father—former Orioles manager Cal Ripken, Sr. Then Cal Ripken, Jr., spoke to the crowd:

"I know that if Lou Gehrig is looking down on tonight's activities, he isn't concerned about someone playing one more consecutive game than he did. Instead, he's viewing tonight as just another example of what is good and right about the American game."[2]

To the surprise of many, Ripken began to jog around the field. He shook hands with and said hello to the fans, groundskeepers, police, and ballpark personnel. Ripken had always taken time out for his fans and for the "little" people around each stadium. Now he was sharing his moment with the Camden Yards fans and with fans everywhere. People knew Ripken's actions were genuine, and they added to the excitement of the event. It was a magical moment, one of the most glorious in sports history.

"This Man Stands Alone"

"Thirty years from now," said former Orioles manager Earl Weaver, "there may be a kid going to bed and dreaming about playing 2,131 games like Cal Ripken did. I mean, talk about role models. This is one of a kind. This man stands alone."[3]

Hall of Fame first baseman George Sisler batted .420 in 1922 for the St. Louis Browns, which would eventually become the Baltimore Orioles.

BEFORE BALTIMORE

Today's Baltimore Orioles can trace their heritage to not one, but two baseball franchises.

Baltimore's First Team

Back in the 1890s, another Baltimore team called the Orioles played in the National League. The "Old Orioles" were tough competitors, who would do anything to win. Historians rate them among the greatest teams of the nineteenth century. The team's roster included these Hall of Famers: third baseman John McGraw, catcher Wilbert Robinson, pitcher Joe "Iron Man" McGinnity, shortstop Hughie Jennings, and outfielders Wee Willie Keeler and Joe Kelley. Under manager Ned Hanlon (another Hall of Famer), they won National League pennants in 1894, 1895, and 1896. Orioles attendance, however, was poor (121,935 in 1899), and after the 1899 season the team disbanded.

Soon afterward, a new major league, the American League (AL), began operating. The AL also had a franchise called the Baltimore Orioles. League president Ban Johnson thought it was more important for his league to have a franchise in New York City. As a result, in 1903, the Baltimore Orioles became the New York Highlanders—and eventually the New York Yankees.

A Move to St. Louis

The original AL also had a franchise in Milwaukee. In 1901 the Brewers finished eighth (dead last) and drew just 139,034 fans. The following year the club moved to St. Louis and changed its nickname to the Browns. This is the team that would become today's Baltimore Orioles.

The Browns were just plain bad. In their history (1902–53), they won 3,414 games but lost 4,465. They finished last eleven times, seventh twelve times, and in sixth place eleven times.

At first the Browns were not too bad. They finished second in 1902, but had only three winning seasons between 1903 and 1920. In the 1920s, however, the team enjoyed a burst of glory. Assisted by such stars as Hall of Fame first baseman George Sisler, pitcher Urban Shocker, and slugging outfielders Baby Doll Jacobson and Ken Williams, the Browns began to improve dramatically. In 1922, Sisler hit .420, Shocker won 24 games, and Williams led the American League with 39 home runs and 155 RBIs. The Browns finished just one game behind the New York Yankees, but after that season it was all downhill. Sisler developed a sinus infection in January 1923, which eventually affected his vision. After that he never saw the ball as well, and could not hit as well. The Browns began sliding toward the bottom of the standings.

Disappointing Seasons

Partly because of the Great Depression, in 1935 the team drew only 80,922 to Sportsman's Park, its home field. In 1937, the Browns lost 108 games; in 1939, 111 games. Occasionally, the team had quality players such as pitchers "Bobo" Newsom and Elden Auker or steady third baseman Harlond Clift. Usually the team's players were pretty terrible.

In 1941, the team was on the verge of moving to Los Angeles. The Japanese attacked the American naval base at Pearl Harbor that December, bringing the United States into World War II. Because of the war, the American League canceled the Browns' plans to move. For the war, the United States government increased the size of its military by holding a draft to select people to serve the country. Many of baseball's best players had to be drafted into the armed services.

The Browns, which had many of baseball's worst players, suddenly found the competition to be more equal. In 1944, the team vaulted from sixth place to first. Led by slugging shortstop Vern Stephens, who led the American League with 109 runs batted in, and pitcher Jack Kramer (17–13), the Browns faced the St. Louis Cardinals in that fall's World Series. The Browns lost to the Cards in six games.

Attempts to Bring in Fans

When the war ended, the Browns returned to normal, actually to worse than normal. Attendance faltered and the club sold Stephens and Kramer to the Boston Red Sox. The team lost 101 games in 1949, and 102 games in 1951. That season, flamboyant baseball executive Bill Veeck bought the club. He tried everything he could to boost attendance, including hiring three-foot seven-inch Eddie Gaedel to play for the Browns, but nothing worked. The team finished 54–100 in 1953. Things were so bad that in its last game, the team exhausted its supply of clean baseballs

In 1951, St. Louis Browns owner Bill Veeck hired three-foot seven-inch Eddie Gaedel to boost attendance. He drew a walk in his only plate appearance.

The Orioles moved to Baltimore prior to the start of the 1954 season. Their current stadium, Oriole Park at Camden Yards, opened in 1992.

and had to play with a used ball. After the game, St. Louis fans were extremely upset with Veeck. Two days later, Veeck sold the club to a group of Baltimore investors for $2.475 million. That same day, the American League approved transferring the franchise to Baltimore.

The St. Louis Browns were no more. The latest version of the Baltimore Orioles had just begun.

Before Baltimore

Many experts believe Brooks Robinson is the greatest fielding third baseman ever. Here, he catches a line drive off the bat of Johnny Bench in Game 5 of the 1970 World Series.

ORIOLES IMMORTALS

The Orioles have boasted many fine players in their long history. The following players either have been inducted into Baseball's Hall of Fame—or, in the case of Cal Ripken, Jr.—will be:

Brooks Robinson

Most observers still regard Brooks Robinson as the finest fielding third baseman ever to play the game. Beginning in 1960, Robinson captured sixteen straight Gold Glove Awards, a number equaled only by pitcher Jim Kaat. The 1970 World Series saw Robinson at his best, as he turned great play after great play.

Although not remembered as a super hitter, in 1964 Robinson batted .317 with 28 homers and a league-leading 118 RBIs. That production gave him AL MVP (Most Valuable Player) honors.

"I once thought of giving him some tips," Hall of Fame third baseman Pie Traynor once revealed, "but dropped the idea. Robinson is wonderful on every type of play. He's just the best there is."[1]

Frank Robinson

When Frank Robinson joined the Orioles, he had already established himself as a star with the Cincinnati Reds, winning National League MVP honors in 1961. After the Reds traded Robinson to Baltimore following the 1965 season, Reds general manager Bill DeWitt implied Robinson was just about washed up.

Robinson was not pleased. In his first season with the Orioles, he responded by winning the AL Triple Crown with 49 homers, 122 RBIs, and a .316 average. Once again, he captured MVP honors. He paced Baltimore to their first AL pennant and a World Series sweep over the Dodgers.

In his first year of eligibility, 1982, Robinson won election to the Baseball Hall of Fame.

Luis Aparicio

Luis Aparicio was perhaps the finest shortstop of his era. The Venezuelan native never hit for great average or power, but it was not his hitting that made him a Hall of Famer. He led the American League in stolen bases in his first nine AL seasons. He also won nine Gold Glove Awards and captured 1956 AL Rookie of the Year honors.

In 1959, he helped lead the Chicago White Sox to their first pennant in forty years. He joined the Orioles

After he was traded from the Reds to the Orioles, Frank Robinson won the American League Triple Crown in 1966.

in 1963, and it is no accident that they won a world championship in 1966. Aparicio won election to the Hall of Fame in 1984.

Jim Palmer

How good was Jim Palmer? His lifetime 268–152 record translated into an impressive .638 won-lost percentage. Eight times, he won 20 or more games—only one of three American League pitchers to accomplish that feat. In doing so, he earned three Cy Young Awards.

Orioles Immortals

Jim Palmer is one of only three American League pitchers to win 20 or more games in a season eight different times. He won three Cy Young Awards.

You would think a pitcher such as Palmer would be a manager's dream, but he and Baltimore manager Earl Weaver feuded constantly. Some thought the pair hated each other. "We didn't," Palmer revealed. "We just loved to play baseball. And hated to lose. And we never quit."[2]

He won election to the Hall of Fame in 1990. He was the third most widely selected pitcher in the history of Hall of Fame voting.

Cal Ripken, Jr.

Shortstop Cal Ripken, Jr., will now always be remembered for his consecutive-games-played streak (2,632 games from 1982 through 1998), but he is much more than that.

He is one of the greatest shortstops of all time. In 1982, he won AL Rookie of the Year honors. In 1983, he helped lead Baltimore to the world championship as he won both the AL MVP Award and *The Sporting News* Player of the Year Award. In 1991, he won both honors again. Ripken won Gold Gloves in 1991 and 1992.

That's impressive enough, but people will also remember Ripken for the type of person he is. His work ethic is outstanding. He is a devoted father and husband, and patiently takes a great deal of time to autograph balls and programs for fans.

In a long line of Orioles heroes, Cal Ripken, Jr., has established himself as the greatest.

Lee MacPhail was one of the Orioles' best general managers. Under his guidance, the Orioles developed talented players such as Brooks Robinson and Boog Powell.

ORIOLES MANAGEMENT

The Orioles have been led by several of baseball's most famous managers and executives. Two—Lee MacPhail and Earl Weaver—are in the Baseball Hall of Fame in Cooperstown.

Paul Richards

He never won a pennant, but many still believe Paul Richards was among the smartest people ever to work in baseball.

From 1955 to 1961, Richards served as Orioles manager and helped develop a strong young pitching staff, known as the "Kiddie Corps." At one point he signed knuckleball pitcher Hoyt Wilhelm. When catcher Gus Triandos had trouble catching the tricky delivery, Richards even invented a special oversized catcher's mitt to solve the problem. His sharp eye for talent helped lay the foundation for Baltimore's fine teams of the 1960s.

Lee MacPhail

Also helping build the Orioles' future was executive Lee MacPhail, son of pioneering Hall of Fame executive Larry MacPhail. After helping build the New York Yankees farm system, MacPhail became Baltimore's general manager in 1958. He helped develop such talent as third baseman Brooks Robinson, pitcher Milt Pappas (later traded to acquire Frank Robinson), and first baseman Boog Powell. The quietly competent MacPhail also acquired shortstop Luis Aparicio and second baseman Davey Johnson.

In 1965, MacPhail left to become assistant to newly elected baseball commissioner William D. Eckert. "Baltimore," said MacPhail, "had been great for my family and for me."[1] In 1974, he became president of the American League and served until 1984. MacPhail was inducted into the Baseball Hall of Fame in 1998. He and his father are the only father-son combination in Cooperstown.

Hank Bauer

The late *Los Angeles Times* columnist Jim Murray once wrote that tough former Yankees outfielder Hank Bauer had a "face [that looked] like a closed fist."[2] Bauer played hard and managed hard. He became an Orioles coach in 1963 and took over as manager the following year. In 1966, he delivered the club's first world championship. In 1968, he was replaced as pilot by Coach Earl Weaver at midseason. Bauer had a 407–318 record as Baltimore manager.

The Baltimore Orioles Baseball Team

Earl Weaver

"Earl [Weaver] stuck by his players long after other managers and owners and coaches and players and the guy's own wife and kids had given up on him," Jim Palmer once wrote. "He put guys in the lineup because of what they once did, not what they could still do. . . . He was fiercely loyal to his players. He cared about them. He stood by them."[3]

With Earl Weaver as manager, the Orioles captured one World Series, four pennants, and two division titles.

Orioles Management

Weaver also knew how to get the best out of every man on his team. "He knew how to use all twenty-five men on the roster," said Frank Robinson, "and he wasn't afraid of being criticized for using the twenty-fifth man. He kept everyone relatively happy because you just didn't sit on the bench with Earl—you got to play."[4]

In his two years at the helm, Davey Johnson guided the Orioles to a wild-card berth and a division title. He also won three Gold Glove awards when he played for Baltimore.

Weaver's 1969 team won 109 games and the AL pennant, but lost the World Series to Gil Hodges' Miracle Mets. The following year, Weaver and the Orioles defeated the Cincinnati Reds in the World Series. He won the AL pennant again in 1971, Eastern Division championships in 1973 and 1974, and another AL pennant in 1979. He lost the 1982 AL East race on the last day of the season and retired after that but returned in 1985. His record with the Orioles was 1,480 wins and just 1,060 losses. Weaver was elected to the Hall of Fame in 1996.

Davey Johnson

Wherever Davey Johnson has been, he's been a winner. When he played for the Orioles, he won three Gold Gloves and played on the pennant-winning teams of 1969–71. Johnson managed the New York Mets to a world championship (1986) and a division championship (1988). In 1994, he had the Cincinnati Reds in first place before a strike ended the season. The following year, he recorded an NL West championship.

In his two seasons as Orioles manager, Johnson brought them to a wild-card berth and an AL East Division championship. His teams finished 88–74 in 1996, and 98–64 in 1997.

The acquisition of Gold Glove shortstop Luis Aparicio (left) from the Chicago White Sox helped the Orioles win the World Series in 1966.

A WINNING TRADITION

When the hapless St. Louis Browns moved to Baltimore in 1954, the change in location did not mean the team magically improved. It remained a poor one. Later in the 1950s, General manager Lee MacPhail and field manager Paul Richards put together a core of talented players—namely, third baseman Brooks Robinson, first baseman Boog Powell, and pitchers Jim Palmer, Dave McNally, Wally Bunker, and Stu Miller.

The First Title

MacPhail acquired Gold Glove shortstop Luis Aparicio from the Chicago White Sox and heavy-hitting outfielder Frank Robinson from the Cincinnati Reds. In 1966, the mix of talented veterans and enthusiastic youngsters resulted in an AL pennant. In that fall's World Series, manager Hank Bauer's Baltimore Orioles swept the Dodgers four straight, including three consecutive shutouts. "There was never any doubt in my mind that we would beat them," said Frank Robinson. "I think it just proves that, if you're dedicated to a cause, if you want something badly enough, you can really do it. That was our ball club in 1966, and that was our ball club in the World Series."[1]

"The Oriole Way"

By 1969, the Orioles had a new manager, Earl Weaver, who had been a successful manager in the Baltimore farm system and who had helped develop the method of play known as the "Oriole way." The team won a club-record 109 games. But this time it was their turn to be upset in the World Series, losing in five games to New York's Miracle Mets.

The 1970 Orioles were almost as good as the 1969 team in the regular season—108 wins. That season, first baseman Boog Powell won the AL MVP Award. In that year's Fall Classic the Birds improved on 1969, defeating the Cincinnati Reds in five games.

Pennant Winners

In 1971, the Orioles pitching staff boasted not one—but four—twenty-game winners: Dave McNally, Jim Palmer, Mike Cuellar, and Pat Dobson. That group guided their team to its third straight pennant. "I've got the best damn ball club in the universe," bragged Weaver. "Won over a hundred games three years in a row. Great spirit. Great ability. Great everything."[2] But in the World Series the great Roberto Clemente

Boog Powell (right) joins the celebration after the Orioles won the 1966 World Series. In 1970, Powell was named AL MVP and helped lead the Orioles to another title.

banged out 12 hits, and his Pirates defeated Baltimore in seven games.

Weaver's Orioles captured division titles in both 1973 and 1974. Each year, the team lost the American League Championship Series (ALCS) to the Oakland A's. Baltimore did not win a pennant again until 1979, when they were led by Cy Young Award winner Mike Flanagan, and outfielder Ken Singleton (35 homers and 111 RBIs). Once again, the Orioles lost to Pittsburgh in the World Series.

Eddie Murray hitting his 500th career home run on September 6, 1996. In 1983, when the Orioles defeated the Phillies in the World Series, he hit 33 home runs and collected 111 RBIs.

Cal Ripken, Jr., first came up from the minors in late 1981 and won AL Rookie of the Year honors in 1982. In 1983, he put together an MVP season. He then helped guide the Orioles to victories over the White Sox in the ALCS and over the Phillies in the World Series. Other key Orioles that year included first baseman Eddie Murray (33 HR, 111 RBIs), and pitchers Scott McGregor (18–7) and Tippy Martinez (21 saves).

Broken Wings

Not every Orioles season has been a good one, however. The team lost its last five spring-training games in 1988—then was outscored 53–7 as it lost its first six regular-season contests. Manager Cal Ripken, Sr., was replaced with Frank Robinson. Orioles fans remained supportive, though. They tried everything they could to help their team. The press arrived in droves. "It was like the World Series every night," Orioles broadcaster Jon Miller commented about the massive media attention the team received. "They had 250 people from the media covering the ballclub by then."[3] But the Orioles kept losing, dropping a major-league record 21 straight losses and stumbling to an Orioles-worst 54–107 record.

The following year the Orioles bounced back strong, leading the American League East for 117 days and moving up to second place with an 87–75 record.

The Orioles were ready for a new decade of competition.

Center fielder Brady Anderson hit a club-record 50 home runs in 1996. His previous career high was 21 home runs.

6

ROLLER-COASTER CHANGE

The 1990s began slowly for the Orioles. Under managers Frank Robinson and Johnny Oates, Baltimore finished no higher than second place from 1990 through 1994. This was in spite of an MVP season from Cal Ripken, Jr., in 1991.

A New Home

Not even the opening of beautiful new Oriole Park at Camden Yards seemed to make much of a difference. On April 6, 1992, the Orioles moved from Memorial Stadium, the team's home since moving to Baltimore in 1954 to Camden Yards. The new complex combined a traditional look with modern conveniences. Built in downtown Baltimore, near the historic brick B & O (Baltimore & Ohio Railroad) warehouse and the exciting Inner Harbor area, fans flocked to it. Since then, Camden Yards has inspired many imitations. These include Jacobs Field, Coors Field, and The

Ballpark in Arlington. "Camden Yards," says ballparks historian Michael Gershman, "is clearly the most innovative and influential major league ballpark designed since Yankee Stadium."[1]

High-Powered Attack

In 1996, Davey Johnson, a highly successful former National League manager, took over Baltimore's managerial reins. The Orioles hit a major-league record 257 home runs. This included a club-record 50 by outfielder Brady Anderson, 39 by first baseman Rafael Palmeiro, and 28 by outfielder-third baseman Bobby Bonilla. Baltimore finished second (88–74) in the AL East, four games back of the Yankees. At one point the Orioles lost 51 of 91 games and seemed out of the race. General manager Pat Gillick tried to trade players with large salaries such as Bonilla and pitcher David Wells, but owner Peter Angelos resisted. The Orioles rebounded to win 37 of their last 58 games, earning a wild-card berth.

In the AL Division Series, Baltimore defeated Cleveland three games to one. Cal Ripken batted .444 and Eddie Murray hit an even .400. In the ALCS, however, the Yankees trimmed the Birds' wings four games to one. Not helping matters was a controversial call in Game 1. Yankee shortstop Derek Jeter hit a ball that twelve-year-old New York fan Jeffrey Maier deflected. That kept Orioles outfielder Tony Tarasco from catching the ball. Umpire Rich Garcia mistakenly ruled the play a home run, and the Orioles ultimately lost the game 5–4 in 11 innings.

An Inspiration

In 1997, the Orioles finished 98–64, first in the AL East. Baltimore led the division from opening day to season's end. Jimmy Key (16–10), Scott Erickson (16–7), Mike Mussina (15–8), and veteran reliever Randy Myers (45 saves, 1.51 ERA) led the pitching staff. First baseman Rafael Palmeiro hit 38 homers and drove in 110 runs. Outfielder Eric Davis bravely returned from having undergone treatment for cancer and batted .304. "It's a miracle as far as I'm concerned," said Davey Johnson when discussing

B. J. Surhoff (left) and Rafael Palmeiro (right) celebrate a big play. By hitting 39 home runs in 1996, Palmeiro helped the Orioles hit a major-league record 257 homers.

Roller-Coaster Change

In the 1990s Mike Mussina was one of the best pitchers in the major leagues. From 1991 to 1999, he went 136–66 with a 3.50 ERA.

Davis. "He has been an inspiration to all of us. I didn't expect him back in uniform at all this season."[2]

In the AL Division Series, Cal Ripken batted .438, and Baltimore defeated the Seattle Mariners 3–1. In the ALCS, though, the Orioles lost again—this time, four games to two—to Cleveland. Each game Baltimore lost was by a single run.

Some Tough Years

The 1998 season proved to be a major disappointment. After the 1997 season, Johnson was named AL Manager of the Year, but he quarreled with club owner Peter Angelos and quit as manager. Former Orioles pitching coach Ray Miller replaced Johnson, but was unable to equal his winning ways. Baltimore posted a mediocre 79–83 record, failing to make the playoffs. Perhaps the most notable event in the season was Cal Ripken's decision to end his famed playing streak. On September 20, 1998, Ripken sat out his first game since May 29, 1982, after 2,632 straight games.

In 1999, despite Mike Mussina (18–7), Albert Belle (37 HR, 117 RBIs, .297), and B. J. Surhoff (28 HR, 107 RBIs, .308), the Orioles finished a disappointing fourth in the AL East. Mike Hargrove replaced Ray Miller as manager for the 2000 season.

Fans, however, should never count the Orioles out. They have a tradition of winning and a loyal fan base. They will be back.

Roller-Coaster Change

STATISTICS

Team Record

The Orioles History

YEARS	LOCATION	W	L	PCT.	PENNANTS	WORLD SERIES
1901–09	Milwaukee St. Louis*	599	721	.454	None	None
1910–19	St. Louis	597	892	.401	None	None
1920–29	St. Louis	762	769	.498	None	None
1930–39	St. Louis	578	951	.378	None	None
1940–49	St. Louis	698	833	.456	1944	None
1950–59	St. Louis Baltimore**	632	905	.411	None	None
1960–69	Baltimore	911	698	.566	1966, 1969	1966
1970–79	Baltimore	944	656	.590	1970, 1971, 1979	1970
1980–89	Baltimore	800	761	.512	1983	1983
1990–99	Baltimore	794	757	.512	None	None

*The Milwaukee Brewers moved to St. Louis prior to the 1902 season and became the Browns.
**The St. Louis Browns moved to Baltimore prior to the 1954 season and became the Orioles.

The Orioles Today

YEAR	W	L	PCT.	MANAGER	DIVISION FINISH
1990	76	85	.472	Frank Robinson	5
1991	67	95	.414	Frank Robinson Johnny Oates	6
1992	89	73	.549	Johnny Oates	3

The Baltimore Orioles Baseball Team

The Orioles Today (con't)

YEAR	W	L	PCT.	MANAGER	DIVISION FINISH
1993	85	77	.525	Johnny Oates	3
1994	63	49	.563	Johnny Oates	2
1995	71	73	.493	Phil Regan	3
1996	88	74	.543	Davey Johnson	2
1997	98	64	.605	Davey Johnson	1
1998	79	83	.488	Ray Miller	4
1999	78	84	.481	Ray Miller	4

Total History

W	L	PCT.	PENNANTS	WORLD SERIES
7,315	7,943	.479	7	3

W=Wins **L**=Losses **PCT.**=Winning Percentage
PENNANTS= Won League Title **WORLD SERIES**= Won World Series

Championship Managers

MANAGER	YEARS MANAGED	RECORD	CHAMPIONSHIPS
Luke Sewell	1941–46	432–410	American League, 1944
Hank Bauer	1964–68	407–318	World Series, 1966
Earl Weaver	1968–82 1985–86	1,480–1,060	American League, 1969, 1971, 1979 World Series, 1970 AL Eastern Division, 1973–74
Joe Altobelli	1983–85	212–167	World Series, 1983
Davey Johnson	1996–97	186–138	AL Wild-card, 1996 AL Eastern Division, 1997

Statistics

Great Hitters

CAREER STATISTICS

PLAYER	SEA	YRS	G	AB	R	H	HR	RBI	SB	AVG
Paul Blair	1964–76	17	1,947	6,042	776	1,513	134	620	171	.250
Harlond Clift	1934–43	12	1,582	5,730	1,070	1,558	178	829	69	.272
Eddie Murray	1977–88, 1996	21	3,026	11,336	1,627	3,255	504	1,917	110	.287
Rafael Palmeiro	1994–98	14	1,940	7,281	1,157	2,158	361	1,227	86	.296
Boog Powell	1961–74	17	2,042	6,681	889	1,776	339	1,187	20	.266
Cal Ripken, Jr.	1981–99	19	2,790	10,765	1,561	2,991	402	1,571	36	.278
Brooks Robinson*	1955–77	23	2,896	10,654	1,232	2,848	268	1,357	28	.267
Frank Robinson*	1966–71	21	2,808	10,006	1,829	2,943	586	1,812	204	.294
Ken Singleton	1975–84	15	2,082	7,189	985	2,029	246	1,065	21	.282
George Sisler*	1915–22 1924–27	15	2,055	8,267	1,284	2,812	102	1,175	375	.340

SEA=Seasons with Orioles/Browns
YRS=Years in the Majors
G=Games
AB=At-Bats
R=Runs Scored
H=Hits
HR=Home Runs
RBI=Runs Batted In
SB=Stolen Bases
AVG=Batting Average
*Member of National Baseball Hall of Fame

Great Pitchers

CAREER STATISTICS

PLAYER	SEA	YRS	W	L	PCT	ERA	G	SV	IP	K	SH
Dennis Martinez	1976–86	23	245	193	.559	3.70	692	8	3,999	2,149	30
Dave McNally	1962–74	14	184	119	.607	3.24	424	2	2,730	1,512	33
Mike Mussina	1991–99	9	136	66	.673	3.50	254	0	1,772	1,325	14
Jim Palmer*	1965–67 1969–84	19	268	152	.638	2.86	558	4	3,948	2,212	53
Hoyt Wilhelm*	1958–62	21	143	122	.540	2.52	1,070	227	2,254	1,610	5

SEA=Seasons with Orioles
YRS=Years in the Majors
W=Wins
L=Losses
PCT=Winning Percentage
ERA=Earned Run Average
G=Games
SV=Saves
IP=Innings Pitched
K=Strikeouts
SH=Shutouts
*Member of National Baseball Hall of Fame

The Baltimore Orioles Baseball Team

CHAPTER NOTES

Chapter 1. The Iron Man
1. Stew Thornley, *Cal Ripken, Jr.: Oriole Ironman* (Minneapolis: Lerner Publications Co., 1992), p. 10.

2. Dr. James Beckett, ed., *9 Innings with Cal Ripken, Jr.* (Dallas: Beckett, 1998), p. 119.

3. Allan Simpson, ed., *Baseball America's 1996 Almanac* (Durham, N.C.: Baseball America, 1996), p. 11.

Chapter 3. Orioles Immortals
1. Tom Murray, ed., *Sport Magazine's All-Time All Stars* (New York: Atheneum, 1977), p. 45.

2. Jim Palmer and Jim Dale, *Together We Were Eleven Foot Nine: The Twenty-Year Friendship of Hall of Fame Pitcher Jim Palmer & Orioles Manager Earl Weaver* (Kansas City: Andrews McMeel Publishing, 1996), p. 168.

Chapter 4. Orioles Management
1. Lee MacPhail, *My 9 Innings* (Westport, Conn.: Meckler, 1989), p. 79.

2. Paul Dickson, *Baseball's Greatest Quotations* (New York: HarperCollins, 1992), p. 300.

3. Jim Palmer and Jim Dale, *Together We Were Eleven Foot Nine: The Twenty-Year Friendship of Hall of Fame Pitcher Jim Palmer & Orioles Manager Earl Weaver* (Kansas City: Andrews McMeel Publishing, 1996), p. 161.

4. Frank Robinson and Berry Stainback, *Extra Innings* (New York: McGraw Hill, 1988), p. 83.

Chapter 5. A Winning Tradition
1. Frank Robinson with Al Silverman, *My Life Is Baseball* (Garden City, N.Y.: Doubleday, 1968), p. 213.

2. Gene Schoor, *The History of the World Series* (New York: Morrow, 1990), p. 312.

3. George Robinson and Charles Salzberg, *On a Clear Day They Could See Seventh Place: Baseball's Worst Teams* (New York: Dell, 1991), p. 279.

Chapter 6. Roller-Coaster Change
1. Michael Gershman, *Diamonds: The Evolution of the Ballpark* (Boston: Houghton Mifflin, 1993), p. 229.

2. Paul White, ed., *USA Today Baseball Weekly 1998 Almanac* (New York: Henry Holt and Co., 1998), p. 18.

GLOSSARY

American Association—A defunct major league that operated from 1882 to 1891. Not to be confused with a minor league by the same name.

American League—One of the two current major leagues of baseball, founded in 1901 by Ban Johnson.

batting average—Hits divided by at-bats.

Commissioner—Baseball's highest official; the office was established in 1920 and first filled by Judge Kenesaw Mountain Landis.

Cy Young Award—Award given each year to the best pitcher in each major league.

designated hitter—A player who does not take the field during the game, but only bats. The designated hitter (DH) is used only in American League ballparks.

ERA (Earned Run Average)—The number of earned runs times nine, divided by the number of innings pitched.

farm system—The system in which Major League Baseball clubs develop talent through a network of minor-league clubs.

fly ball—A ball hit in the air, as opposed to a ground ball.

free agent—A major-leaguer whose contractual obligations to his old team have expired and who is free to sign with any major-league team.

general manager—The official in charge of a ballclub's business and personnel matters.

Gold Glove Award—Award given annually to the best fielder at each position in both the NL and AL.

Hall of Fame—Located in Cooperstown, N.Y. Induction into the National Baseball Hall of Fame is the highest honor that can be awarded to a professional player, manager, umpire, or executive.

homer—Home run.

infielder—One who plays an infield position: first, second, or third base or shortstop.

League Championship Series—The best-of-seven series that determines the AL and NL champions.

Miracle Mets—The 1969 World Championship New York Mets. Their championship was considered to be a miracle because of the franchise's previous poor record.

MVP Award—Most Valuable Player Award; voted on by members of the Baseball Writers Association of America (BBWAA).

National League—The oldest surviving major league. Founded in 1876 by William Hulbert, and sometimes called the "senior circuit."

pennant—A league championship, alternately called the "flag."

RBI—Run(s) batted in.

Rookie of the Year Award—Award given each year to an outstanding rookie in each major league. It was first awarded in 1947, to the Brooklyn Dodgers' Jackie Robinson.

stolen base—A play in which the base runner advances to another base while the pitcher takes his motion.

wild-card—The non-division winning club with the best won-lost percentage in regular-season play; the wild-card team in each league earns a berth in postseason play.

World Series—The end of the season best-of-seven series that pits the champions of the National and American Leagues against each other.

Glossary

FURTHER READING

Beckett, Dr. James. *9 Innings with Cal Ripken, Jr.* Dallas: Beckett, 1998.

Brandt, Ed. *Rafael Palmeiro: At Home with the Baltimore Orioles.* Elkton, Md.: Mitchell Lane, 1997.

Campbell, Jim. *Cal Ripken, Jr.* Broomall, Pa.: Chelsea House Publishers, 1997.

Colston, Chris. *Rare Birds: A Look at the Baltimore Orioles from A to Z.* Lenexa, Kans.: Addax Publishing Group, 1998.

Gershman, Michael. *Diamonds: The Evolution of the Ballpark.* Boston: Houghton Mifflin, 1993.

Joseph, Paul. *Baltimore Orioles* (America's Game). Minneapolis: Abdo & Daughters, 1997.

Macnow, Glenn. *Sports Great Cal Ripken, Jr.* Berkeley Heights, N.J.: Enslow, 1993.

Palmer, Jim, and Jim Dale. *Together We Were Eleven Foot Nine: The Twenty-Year Friendship of Hall of Fame Pitcher Jim Palmer and Orioles Manager Earl Weaver.* Kansas City: Andrews McMeel Publishing, 1996.

Patterson, Ted, and Brooks Robinson. *The Baltimore Orioles: Forty Years of Magic from 33rd Street to Camden Yards.* Dallas: Taylor Publishing, 1994.

Pluto, Terry, *The Earl of Baltimore.* Piscataway, N.J.: New Century, 1982.

Ripken, Cal, with Mike Bryan. *The Only Way I Know.* New York: Penguin USA, 1998.

Robinson, Frank, and Berry Stainback. *Extra Innings.* New York: McGraw Hill, 1988.

Savage, Jeff. *Cal Ripken, Jr.: Star Shortstop.* Springfield, N.J.: Enslow, 1994.

Thornley, Stew. *Cal Ripken, Jr.: Oriole Ironman.* Minneapolis: Lerner Publications Co., 1992.

Thorn, John, et. al. *Total Baseball: The Official Encyclopedia of Major League Baseball.* 6th ed. New York: Total Sports, 1999.

INDEX

A
Alexander, Manny, 6, 7
Anderson, Brady, 36
Angelos, Peter, 6, 36, 39
Aparicio, Luis, 18, 24, 29
Auker, Elden, 13

B
Baltimore & Ohio (B&O) Warehouse, 35
Baltimore Orioles (1901–02), 12
Baltimore Orioles (NL), 11
Bauer, Hank, 24, 29
Belle, Albert, 39
Bonilla, Bobby, 36
Bunker, Wally, 29

C
Clemente, Roberto, 30
Clift, Harlond, 13
Cuellar, Mike, 30

D
Davis, Eric, 37
DeWitt, Bill, 18
Dobson, Pat, 30

E
Easley, Damion, 6
Eckert, William D., 24
Erickson, Scott, 37

F
Flanagan, Mike, 31

G
Gaedel, Eddie, 14
Garcia, Rich, 36
Gehrig, Lou, 5, 6, 9
Gershman, Michael, 36
Gillick, Pat, 36

H
Hargrove, Mike, 39
Hanlon, Ned, 11
Hirdt, Steve, 6
Hodges, Gil, 27

J
Jacobson, Baby Doll, 12
Jeter, Derek, 36
Johnson, Ban, 12
Johnson, Davey, 24, 27, 36, 37, 39

K
Kaat, Jim, 17
Keeler, Wee Willie, 11
Kelley, Joe, 11
Key, Jimmy, 37
"Kiddie Corps," 23
Kramer, Jack, 13, 14

L
Los Angeles Times, 24

M
MacPhail, Larry, 24
MacPhail, Lee, 23, 24, 29
Maier, Jeffrey, 36
Martinez, Tippy, 33
McGinnity, Joe "Iron Man," 11
McGraw, John, 11
McGregor, Scott, 33
McNally, Dave, 29, 30
Miller, Jon, 33
Miller, Ray, 39
Miller, Stu, 29
Milwaukee Brewers (1901), 12
Murray, Eddie, 33, 36
Murray, Jim, 24
Mussina, Mike, 37, 39
Myers, Randy, 37

N
New York Highlanders, 12
New York Mets, 27, 30
New York Yankees, 12, 24, 36
Newsom, "Bobo," 13

Index

O

Oates, Johnny, 35
Oriole Park at Camden Yards, 6, 9, 35, 36

P

Palmeiro, Raphael, 36, 37
Palmer, Jim, 19, 21, 25, 29, 30
Pappas, Milt, 24
Philadelphia Phillies, 33
Powell, Boog, 24, 29, 30

R

Richards, Paul, 23 , 29
Ripken, Cal, Jr., 5–7, 9, 17, 21, 33, 35, 36, 39
Ripken, Cal, Sr., 9, 33
Robinson, Brooks, 17–18, 24, 29
Robinson, Frank, 18, 24, 26, 29, 30, 33, 35
Robinson, Wilbert, 11

S

St. Louis Browns (1902–53), 12–15, 29
St. Louis Cardinals, 13
Shocker, Urban, 12
Singleton, Ken, 31
Sisler, George, 12–13
Sporting News, The, 21
Sportsman's Park, 13
Stephens, Vern, 13, 14
Surhoff, B. J., 39

T

Tarasco, Tony, 36
Traynor, Pie, 18
Triandos, Gus, 23

V

Veeck, Bill, 14, 15

W

Weaver, Earl, 9, 21, 23, 24, 25–26, 30, 31, 41
Wells, David, 36
Wilhelm, Hoyt, 23, 42
Williams, Ken, 12

WHERE TO WRITE

Baltimore Orioles
333 West Camden Street
Baltimore, MD 21201

WEB SITES

http://www.TheOrioles.com
http://www.majorleaguebaseball.com/u/baseball/mlb/teams/BAL/index.html

DATE DUE

OCT 24 2001		
OCT 26 2001		
DEC 17 2002		
JAN 07 2004		
DEC 02 2004		
JAN 20 2006		
MAR 20 2007		
NOV 09 2007		
NOV 11 2008		
SEP 11 2009		
FEB 21 2011		

FOLLETT